LAUGH
-Out-
LOUD
HOLIDAY
JOKES
for KIDS

LAUGH -Out- LOUD HOLIDAY JOKES for KIDS

2-IN-1 COLLECTION OF SPOOKY JOKES AND CHRISTMAS JOKES

ROB ELLIOTT

HARPER

An Imprint of HarperCollins Publishers

ISBN 978-0-06-256976-9

Typography by Gearbox
17 18 19 20 PC/RRDH   10 9 8 7 6 5 4 3
❖
First Edition

LAUGH
-Out-
LOUD
HOLIDAY
JOKES
for KIDS

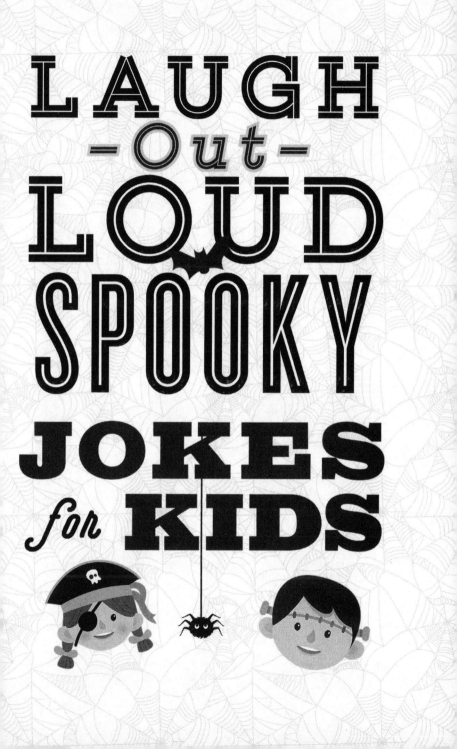

LAUGH
-Out-
LOUD
SPOOKY
JOKES for KIDS

Q: What kind of music do mummies like to listen to?

A: Wrap music

Q: Why did Dracula go to the doctor?

A: Because he couldn't stop coffin.

Q: Why do ghosts make horrible fans?

A: Because they're always booing!

Q: What monster is the best at hide-and-seek?

A: A where-wolf

Q: Who is the smartest monster of all?

A: Frank-Einstein

Q: Why did the ghost need a tissue?

A: Because he had a lot of boo-gers.

Q: What kind of bug will never die?

A: A zom-bee

Q: Who was the most famous painter

   of monsters?

A: Vincent van Ghost

Q: How can you tell when a

   mummy is stressed out?

A: It gets unraveled.

Q: What is a spider's favorite workout?

A: A spin class

Q: Why can't you ever tell a skeleton a secret?

A: Because it just goes in one ear and out the other.

Q: Why didn't the skeleton cross the road?

A: He didn't have the guts.

Q: What's a witch's favorite subject?

A: Spell-ing

Q: What do you get when you mix a vampire and a baseball?

A: A baseball bat

Q: What kind of monster lives in a tissue?

A: The boogey-man

Q: What do you call a pretty ghost?

A: Boo-tiful

Q: What kind of dog does Dracula own?

A: A bloodhound

Q: What kind of bird is the spookiest?

A: The scarecrow

Q: What do you call a field full of eyeballs?

A: An eye patch

Q: What kind of eggs do monsters eat?

A: Deviled eggs

Q: What happened to the monster when he ate his vegetables and got lots of sleep?

A: He grew-some.

Q: What does a vampire eat for dinner?

A: Mashed potatoes and grave-y

Q: What does a skeleton wear for Halloween?

A: A cos-tomb

Q: **What do you get when a monster goes to the bathroom?**

A: Cree-pee

Q: **Which monster is the heaviest?**

A: A skele-ton

Q: **What is a monster's favorite dessert?**

A: Ice scream

Q: **What did one casket say to the other casket?**

A: "Is that you coffin?"

Q: **What do monsters put in their chili?**

A: Human bean-ings

Q: What do canaries say on Halloween?

A: "Trick or tweet"

Q: Which room is missing in a ghost's house?

A: The living room

Q: How do you watch a scary movie on Halloween?

A: On your flat-scream TV

Q: What do you call an undercover bug?

A: A spy-der

Knock, knock.

Who's there?

Autumn.

Autumn who?

We autumn make some pumpkin pie.

Tongue Twisters—Say each one ten times fast!

Black cats.

Ghosts glow.

Pumpkin pie, please.

Plump pumpkins.

Knock, knock.

Who's there?

Leaf.

Leaf who?

Leaf me some of your Halloween candy.

Q: What is a monster's favorite book?

A: *Little House on the Scary*

Q: Why were the monster's pants too short?

A: Because he grew-some.

Q: What kind of monster do you see on the dance floor?

A: A boogie-man

Q: What do you get when you cross a ghoul and a turkey?

A: A gobble-in

Q: What is a ghost's favorite treat?

A: Boo-berry pie

Q: What does a skeleton say when it goes on a cruise?

A: "Bone voyage."

Q: How do monsters style their hair?

A: With scare spray

Q: Where do ghosts go for spring break?

A: Mali-boo

Q: Why does Dracula have a hard time finding a job?

A: Because he's a pain in the neck.

Q: What is a goblin's favorite ride at the amusement park?

A: The roller ghost-er

Q: How does a ghost unlock its door?

A: With a spoo-key

Q: What kind of ghost always comes back to you?

A: A boo-merang

Knock, knock.

Who's there?

The interrupting ghost.

The inter—

Booooo!

Q: What do werewolves put on their waffles?

A: Whipped scream

**Q: What did the mother ghost say to her
son when he left for summer camp?**

A: "You'll be mist."

Q: What did the witch get at the hotel?

A: Broom service

Q: Why wouldn't the zombie get a job?

A: Because he was a dead-beat!

Q: What instrument does a skeleton play?

A: The trom-bone

Q: Why was the pumpkin afraid to cross the road?

A: It didn't want to get squash-ed.

Q: What did the boy pumpkin say to the girl pumpkin?

A: "You're gourd-geous."

Q: How does a monster like his coffee?

A: With scream and sugar

Q: Why did Dracula die at the restaurant?

A: He ordered the chicken-fried stake!

Q: Where do zombies buy their snacks?

A: At the gross-ery store

Q: Why are skeletons lonely on Valentine's Day?

A: Because they don't have a heart.

Knock, knock.

Who's there?

Justin.

Justin who?

You're Justin time to go trick-or-treating

with me.

Q: What does a ghost wear to the beach?

A: A boo-kini

Q: How do monsters protect their skin at the beach?

A: Sun scream

Q: What do you play with a baby ghost?

A: Peeka-boo

Q: Why do mummies eat pickles?

A: So there's never a dill moment.

Q: What do witches order at the coffee shop?

A: Hocus mochas

Q: What do scarecrows wear to parties?

A: Har-vests

Knock, knock.

Who's there?

Yam.

Yam who?

I yam going to the Halloween party. Are you?

Q: What did the squash say to the

jack-o-lantern?

A: "I yam your best friend."

Knock, knock.

Who's there?

Skeleton.

Skeleton who?

No-body is here right now!

Q: What is the best way to find out about spooky spiders?

A: On a web-site

Q: What do wizards eat for lunch?

A: Sand-witches

Q: What do mummies drink?

A: Ghoul-Aid

Knock, knock.

Who's there?

Dishes.

Dishes who?

Dishes the best these Halloween jokes

are going to get.

Q: Who did the ghost take to the party?

A: His ghoul-friend

Q: What did the skeleton say to

the invisible man?

A: "Long time no see."

Knock, knock.

Who's there?

Irish.

Irish who?

Irish you a Happy Halloween!

Q: Where does Dracula keep his money?

A: In the blood bank

Q: What do you get when you cross a werewolf and an owl?

A: A hoooooowl

Q: What is a math teacher's favorite dessert?

A: Pumpkin pi

Q: Where do skeletons live?

A: On dead-end streets

Q: What do ghosts eat for lunch?

A: Ham-boo-gers and french fries

Q: Why was the pumpkin depressed?

A: It felt all hollow inside.

Q: What game do monsters like to play?

A: Hide-and-shriek

Knock, knock.

Who's there?

Wanda.

Wanda who?

I Wanda suck your blood. . . .

Mwa-hahahaha . . .

Q: What do you get when you combine a ghost and a chicken?

A: A poultry-geist

Q: Where do ghosts like to go swimming?

A: In the Dead Sea

Q: Why did the mummy go on vacation?

A: Because he was all wound up.

Q: What happens when you get kissed by a vampire?

A: Well, I hear it's a pain in the neck!

Q: Why are ghosts such bad liars?

A: Because you can see right through them!

Q: What do you get when you cross Dracula and a snowman?

A: Frostbite

Q: What is a monster's motto?

A: "Eat, drink, and be scary."

Q: How did Dracula fall in love with his girlfriend?

A: All she had to do was bat her eyes.

Q: What do sea monsters eat for dinner?

A: Fish and ships

Q: What do goblins wear trick-or-treating?

A: Cos-tombs

Q: What do you call a werewolf with a camera?

A: A paw-parazzo

Q: How do wizards turn on lights?

A: With light s-witches

Q: What did the baby monster say to its dad?

A: "Where is mummy?"

Q: How do you decide which pie to make for Thanksgiving?

A: You weigh the pros and pe-cons.

Q: What do you call a skeleton that won't work?

A: Lazy-bones

Q: Which monster do you see during the holidays?

A: Santa Claws

Q: What did the boy ghost say to the girl ghost?

A: "You look boo-tiful tonight."

Q: What do you get if you give a black cat a lemon?

A: A sour puss

Q: What does a baby ghost like to wear?

A: Boo-ties

Q: What do you call it when monsters go to dinner and a movie?

A: Intimi-dating

Q: **Why are monsters messy eaters?**

A: Because they're always goblin.

Q: **Why was the vampire a sad vegetarian?**

A: Because you can't get blood out of a turnip.

Q: **What do you get if you have 3.14 pumpkins?**

A: Pumpkin pi

Q: **Why did the monster need dental floss?**

A: He had someone stuck in his teeth.

Q: **What is Frankenstein's favorite food at a cookout?**

A: Hallo-weenies

Knock, knock.

Who's there?

Ben.

Ben who?

Ben wanting to go trick-or-treating for a while now.

Q: Why is Dracula so easy to trick on Halloween?

A: Because he's a sucker.

Q: What do you call two tarantulas when they get married?

A: Newly-webs

Knock, knock.

Who's there?

Shellfish.

Shellfish who?

Don't be shellfish with your Halloween candy.

Knock, knock.

Who's there?

Juicy.

Juicy who?

Did juicy my fun Halloween costume?

Q: What does a skeleton say before he sits down to eat?

A: "Bone appetit."

Q: Why did Dracula ask for a piece of gum?

A: Because he had bat breath.

Leah: Why do witches fly on brooms?

Mason: The cord was too short to ride a

vacuum cleaner.

Q: How do ghosts wash their hair?

A: With sham-boo

Knock, knock.

Who's there?

Wanda.

Wanda who?

I Wanda wish you a Happy Halloween.

- -

Q: What kind of cologne do

   jack-o'-lanterns wear?

A: Pumpkin spice

Q: What kind of pants do ghosts wear?

A: Boo jeans

Knock, knock.

   Who's there?

Needle.

   Needle who?

I needle little more time to come up with a

   Halloween costume.

Q: What kind of cars do goblins drive?

A: Monster trucks

Q: What do you call a ghost up your nose?

A: A boo-ger

Q: How do you fix a hole in your pumpkin?

A: With a pumpkin patch

Knock, knock.

Who's there?

Noah.

Noah who?

Noah good place to trick-or-treat around here?

Q: What is a zombie's favorite treat for Halloween?

A: Butter-fingers

Q: What do swamp monsters eat?

A: Marsh-mallows

Q: What happens when you hit a pumpkin with your car?

A: It gets squashed!

Q: What do zombies eat for breakfast?

A: Bacon and legs

Q: What happened when the girl swallowed her apple juice?

A: It was in-cider.

Q: How did Frankenstein feel on vacation?

A: Like he didn't have a scare in the world

Q: What do witches do when they're tired?

A: They sit for a spell.

Q: What is a zombie's favorite kind of cheese?

A: Limb-burger

Q: Who helped the Bride of Frankenstein go to the ball?

A: Her scary godmother

Q: What did one candy apple say to the other?

A: "Let's stick together."

Q: What do you call a dentist who cleans a vampire's teeth?

A: CRAZY!

Q: How did the monster feel when he was struck by lightning?

A: He was shocked!

Josh: Should I tell the police that we saw a mummy?

Jeff: No, I would keep it under wraps!

Q: What is it like to find a skeleton in the freezer?

A: Bone-chilling

Q: What do werewolves think of vampires?

A: They think they're fang-tastic.

Joe: How was the Halloween party?

Sam: It was spook-tacular!

Q: What do you get when you put a pumpkin in a bag?

A: A sack-o-lantern

Q: What's the scariest kind of horse?

A: A night-mare

Q: What do monsters do with their mouthwash?

A: They gargoyle it!

Q: Why was the Creature from the Black Lagoon too busy to go to the Halloween party?

A: He was swamped!

Q: What do you get when you cross a snake and a ghost?

A: A boo-a constrictor

Anna: How much does that tombstone weigh?

Emma: A skele-ton

Q: What kind of boat does Dracula have?

A: A blood vessel

Q: What happens when an ogre eats beans?

A: It's gas-tly.

Q: Why was the gremlin afraid of the goblin's dog?

A: It was pet-rifying.

Q: Who won't drink milk on Halloween?

A: Cow-ards

Q: What is it like to listen to Dracula's heartbeat?

A: Re-pulse-ive

Q: What do you get when you cross a werewolf with a pine tree?

A: A monster whose bark is worse than its bite

Q: What is a vampire's favorite fruit?

A: Neck-tarines

Q: Where do monsters go sailing?

A: On Lake Eerie

Q: What do you call a vampire who's not very smart?

A: A ding-bat

Knock, knock.

Who's there?

Olive.

Olive who?

Olive this Halloween candy is making me sick!

Q: Where did the police put Dracula in the prison?

A: In a blood cell

Knock, knock.

Who's there?

Wheel.

Wheel who?

Wheel have some fun when we go trick-or-treating tonight.

Q: What kind of car does Dracula drive?

A: A bloodmobile

Q: Why do vampires make good artists?

A: Because they like drawing blood.

Q: Why did the scarecrow win the Nobel Prize?

A: Because he was outstanding in his field.

Q: What does Dracula take when he's got a bad cold?

A: Coffin drops

Q: Why did the cyclops stop teaching math?

A: Because he had only one pupil.

Q: What do ghosts eat for supper?

A: S-boo-ghetti

Q: Why didn't the mummy have any friends?

A: He was too wrapped up in himself.

Q: Why couldn't the skeleton stop laughing?

A: Because someone tickled his funny bone.

Q: Why didn't the scarecrow go back for seconds at Thanksgiving dinner?

A: He was already stuffed.

Q: Why don't you want to go into business with a zombie?

A: It will cost you an arm and a leg.

Knock, knock.

Who's there?

Owl.

Owl who?

Happy owl-oween!

Q: Why did the ghost go to the psychiatrist?

A: He felt like a no-body.

Q: What is a scarecrow's favorite kind of fruit?

A: Straw-berries

Q: Why couldn't the jack-o'-lantern scare the trick-or-treaters?

A: It didn't have the guts!

Q: Why did the monster go on a diet?

A: He was having trouble fitting under the kid's bed.

Q: Why are witches good drivers?

A: They know how to drive a stick.

Q: How did the witch know her potion was mixed right?

A: She used spell check.

Q: What's a ghost's favorite kind of sandwich?

A: Boo-logna and cheese

Q: Where do monsters take their toddlers?

A: To day-scare

Q: Why did the monster order chicken for dinner?

A: He was in a fowl mood.

Q: What happened when the skeleton built a snowman?

A: It chilled him to the bone.

Q: What happened when the turkey got in a fight?

A: He got the stuffing knocked out of him.

Q: What happened when the vampire drank old milk?

A: It was blood-curdling!

Q: Why wouldn't the bull go into the haunted house?

A: Because he was a cow-ard.

Q: What's a zombie's favorite kind of tea?

A: Nas-tea!

Q: Why don't vampires wear shoes?

A: Because they have no souls.

Knock, knock.

Who's there?

Sharon.

Sharon who?

I'm Sharon my Halloween candy with you if you open the door!

Q: What does a monster say when he goes trick-or-treating?

A: "Trick or Eat!"

Q: Where do you go if there is a monster under your bed?

A: To a hotel for the night

Q: Why did the vampire join the circus?

A: He was an acro-bat.

Knock, knock.

Who's there?

Bacon.

Bacon who?

I'm bacon a pumpkin pie. Want some?

Knock, knock.

Who's there?

Funnel.

Funnel who?

The funnel start as soon as you put on your costume!

Knock, knock.

Who's there?

Norway.

Norway who?

There's Norway I'm going to miss Halloween!

Knock, knock.

Who's there?

Count.

Count who?

Count Dracula!

Q: What happened when the duck saw the ghost?

A: He was quacking in his boots!

Q: Why shouldn't you bother a corpse?

A: You might get on their last nerve.

Q: Why did Dracula eat the lightbulb?

A: He wanted a light lunch.

Q: Who helped the pumpkins cross the road?

A: The crossing gourds

- -

Q: Where do zombies like to play?

A: In their graveyard

Knock, knock.

Who's there?

Lego.

Lego who?

Don't Lego of your Halloween candy or

you might lose it.

Q: Why don't you let vampires join the choir?

A: They're always sharp!

Knock, knock.

Who's there?

Phillip.

Phillip who?

Phillip my bag with more candy, please!

Q: What do you get when you cross a monkey and a vampire?

A: An orangu-fang

Q: Why did the mother ghost give her child a time-out?

A: He just wouldn't boo-have.

Q: What did one leaf say to the other leaf?

A: "I think I'm falling for you."

Q: What is a werewolf's favorite breakfast?

A: Pigs in a blanket

Q: Why did the turkey cross the road?

A: To prove it wasn't a chicken!

Q: What do ghosts like to put in their cereal?

A: Boo-nanas

Knock, knock.

Who's there?

Pumpkin.

Pumpkin who?

A pumpkin fill up the flat tire on your bike.

Knock, knock.

Who's there?

Butter.

Butter who?

I butter get a bigger bag for all my

Halloween candy!

Q: How did the turkey get across the lake?

A: He used a gravy boat.

Knock, knock.

Who's there?

Howl.

Howl who?

Howl we wait until next year to go trick-or-treating again?

Knock, knock.

Who's there?

Annie.

Annie who?

Annie body want to go with me to get my Halloween costume?

Q: What is a monster's favorite kind of treat?

A: Ghoul Scout cookies

Q: What is the difference between a werewolf and a cow?

A: One howls at the moon, and one jumps over the moooo-n.

Q: What do you call a bird with a high IQ?

A: Owl-bert Einstein

Q: What do scarecrows use to eat?

A: A pitchfork

Q: What skeleton solves mysteries?

A: Sherlock Bones

Knock, knock.

Who's there?

Emma.

Emma who?

Emma little sick from all this Halloween candy.

Q: What do sea monsters take when they have a cold?

A: Vitamin sea

Q: Why did the young spider get grounded?

A: He was spending too much time on the web.

Q: Why did Dracula's son wake up in the middle of the night?

A: He had a bite-mare.

Q: Why did the vampire forget his cape at home?

A: Because he was going batty.

Q: What do you get when you combine a bear and a ghost?

A: Winnie the Boo

Knock, knock.

Who's there?

Candy.

Candy who?

Candy be time for Halloween already?

Q: What is a turkey's favorite dessert?

A: Apple gobbler

Q: Where does Dracula go when he visits New York City?

A: The Vampire State Building

Q: What does a zombie call a race car driver?

A: Fast food

Q: What does a cow like to dress up as for Halloween?

A: A mooo-vie star

Q: Why can't you invite an optometrist to your Halloween party?

A: Because she'll make a spectacle of herself.

Q: **What do you get when you cross a monkey and a ghost?**

A: A ba-boo-n

Q: **Where did the werewolf keep his coat?**

A: In his claw-set

Q: **Why don't clumsy people like autumn?**

A: They're afraid they'll fall.

Knock, knock.

Who's there?

Dubai.

Dubai who?

We need Dubai some more Halloween candy.

Knock, knock.

Who's there?

Muffin.

Muffin who?

Muffin is going to stop me from trick-or-treating this year.

Q: Why are bats so lazy?

A: Because they just hang around all the time.

Q: What is a monster's favorite musical?

A: *Phantom of the Opera*

Knock, knock.

Who's there?

Avery.

Avery who?

Avery Happy Halloween to everybody!

Knock, knock.

Who's there?

Berry.

Berry who?

I'm berry glad that fall is here.

Q: What do vampires do with their buddies?

A: They fang out!

Q: What kind of coffee does a wizard like?

A: Dark brew

Q: What happened when the vampires had a race?

A: They were neck and neck the whole time.

Knock, knock.

Who's there?

Otter.

Otter who?

You otter carve your pumpkin before Halloween.

Knock, knock.

Who's there?

Bat.

Bat who?

I bat you're going to open the door

on Halloween.

Q: What did the werewolf do after he was

told a joke?

A: He howled with laughter.

Q: Why wouldn't you want to make a

witch mad?

A: Because they're always

flying off the handle.

Knock, knock.

Who's there?

Moe.

Moe who?

I want Moe Halloween candy!

Knock, knock.

Who's there?

Weird.

Weird who?

Weird all my Halloween candy go?

Knock, knock.

Who's there?

Police.

Police who?

Police come to my Halloween party!

Q: What does the caretaker think of
the cemetery?

A: He really digs it!

Q: What is Dracula's favorite kind of soup?

A: Alpha-bat soup

Knock, knock.

Who's there?

Juicy.

Juicy who?

Did juicy my new Halloween costume?

Knock, knock.

Who's there?

Orange.

Orange who?

Orange you glad it's Halloween?

Knock, knock.

Who's there?

Howl.

Howl who?

Howl I get my Halloween candy if you don't open the door?

Q: What do you get when you cross a werewolf and a forest?

A: A fur tree

Knock, knock.

Who's there?

Latte.

Latte who?

It's a latte fun going trick-or-treating with you.

Q: What's a black cat's favorite dessert?

A: Mice cream

Knock, knock.

Who's there?

Candice.

Candice who?

Candice Halloween party be any more fun?

Knock, knock.

Who's there?

Oswald.

Oswald who?

Oswald my Halloween candy and it got stuck in my throat!

Q: Why did Frankenstein stop going to the gym?

A: Because it wasn't working out.

Q: How did the zombie write a book?

A: He hired a ghost writer.

Q: What is a ghost's favorite amusement park ride?

A: The scary-go-round

Q: What kind of cheese did the goblin put on his pizza?

A: Munster cheese

Q: What do ghosts do in their spare time?

A: They read boo-ks.

Q: Why did Dracula get tricked out of

   his lollipops?

A: Because he's a sucker.

Q: What is a monster's favorite dinner dish?

A: Fettuccine Afraid-o

Q: When do ghosts like to go for walks?

A: Sometime in the moaning

Q: What's black, white, and red all over?

A: Dracula with a sunburn

Q: What do you get when a dentist cleans a zombie's teeth?

A: A brush with death

Q: How do zombies like their steak?

A: Very, very rare

Q: What do you call a black cat that has eight legs and likes to swim?

A: An octo-puss

Q: What did the zombie say when it looked in my closet?

A: "I wouldn't be caught dead in these clothes!"

Q: What kind of monster is always alert?

A: An aware-wolf

Q: What kind of parties do monsters like to go to?

A: Ma-scare-ade parties

Knock, knock.

Who's there?

Andy.

Andy who?

Andy-body want to go to the costume party with me?

Q: Why did Jimmy bury his flashlight in the cemetery?

A: The batteries were dead.

Q: Why can't a monster eat more than three dentists?

A: Because they're so filling.

Q: Why are pilgrims so popular?

A: Because Plymouth rocks!

Jimmy: How long does it take to read a ghost story?

Johnny: Not long if you book it.

Q: Why was the road so mad at the trick-or-treaters?

A: They kept crossing it.

Q: Why can't you trust the swamp monster?

A: There's something fishy about him.

Q: What do you get if you throw four zombies in a lake?

A: Cuatro sinko

Q: How do you choose which Halloween candy to buy?

A: It takes a lot of cents.

Q: Why wouldn't the monster eat the clown?

A: He tasted funny.

Jimmy: Your banana costume is ugly!

Johnny: That hurt my peelings!

Q: How did the farmer fix his overalls?

A: With a pumpkin patch

Q: Why couldn't the kid ring the doorbell when he was trick-or-treating?

A: He was a ding-dong.

Q: How did Dracula fix his broken fangs?

A: With tooth-paste

Q: How can I learn more about poisonous spiders?

A: Look it up on a web-site.

Q: Why do we bob for apples on Halloween?

A: Because watermelons are too heavy.

Q: What happened to the chef when he forgot the yams?

A: He got canned.

Q: What kind of flowers bloom on Halloween?

A: Chrysanthe-mums

Jill: I stitched up the hole in your Halloween costume.

Jane: Well, I'll be darned.

Q: Did you hear about the monster who was hit by lightning?

A: It was shocking.

Susie: I think I'll dress up like a lightbulb for Halloween.

Stacy: That's a bright idea!

Q: Why was the witch late for school?

A: Her broom over-swept.

Q: What's a zombie's favorite painting?

A: *The Moan-a Lisa*

Q: What did Godzilla eat for breakfast?

A: A chew-chew train

Joe: Did you find the missing apples from the orchard?

Sam: No. My search was fruitless.

Q: Why is Frankenstein so good at gardening?

A: He has a green thumb.

Mother: We're having your aunt and uncle for Thanksgiving.

Daughter: I was hoping we were having turkey and stuffing.

Q: Why should you dress up as King Arthur for Halloween?

A: You'll be sure to have a good knight.

Q: What runs around a cemetery but never moves?

A: A fence

Q: What do you call a black cat that carries your wallet and keys?

A: A purrrrrse

Q: Why can't you take pigs trick-or-treating?

A: They'll hog all the candy.

Q: What do you call a witch whose broom won't fly?

A: You call a cab.

Q: What is a zombie's favorite game?

A: Swallow the Leader

Q: Why was the pilgrim embarrassed?

A: Because he saw the turkey dressing.

Q: What do you call a witch's lost geometry book?

A: Hex-a-gone

Q: How do you keep monsters out of your closet?

A: Put them under the bed.

Knock, knock.

Who's there?

Harry.

Harry who?

Harry up. It's time to carve our pumpkins!

Joey: Are you charging your flashlight for Halloween?

Jenny: No. I'm paying cash for it.

Q: What happened after the black cats had a fight?

A: They hissed and made up.

Q: Why are werewolves so competitive?

A: It's a dog-eat-dog world out there.

Q: How did the witch stay dry without an umbrella?

A: It wasn't raining.

Q: What do you call a scary dream about a horse?

A: A night-mare

Q: Where do witches buy their pets?

A: From a black cat-alog

Knock, knock.

Who's there?

Luke.

Luke who?

Luke at all the candy I got for Halloween!

Q: Why did the pie crust go to the dentist?

A: Because it needed a filling.

Q: What happens when a monster shows up in the barnyard?

A: It's udder chaos.

Q: What is the silliest Halloween candy?

A: Candy corn-y

Q: **What do black cats have that no other animals have?**

A: Kittens

Q: **What do you get when you cross a skeleton and a trumpet?**

A: A trom-bone

Q: **Did you hear the story about the giant?**

A: It was a tall tale.

Q: **What do you get when you cross a werewolf and a clock?**

A: A watchdog

Q: What do you give a monster for Halloween?

A: Whatever he wants!

Q: How do you make a pineapple shake?

A: You tell it a ghost story!

Q: Where do horses go trick-or-treating?

A: All over the neigh-borhood

Betty: I'm wearing a Mona Lisa costume for Halloween.

Bailey: You'll be pretty as a picture.

Q: What does a zombie call a black belt?

A: Kung-food

Q: What does a bat do for fun?

A: Hangs out with its friends

Q: Why did the witch take a nap?

A: She was hex-austed.

Joe: Why did you put ketchup on your pumpkin pie?

John: Because we're all out of mustard.

Ella: Is that a real photo of Bigfoot hanging on your wall?

Anna: No, it's an im-poster.

Q: How does a ghost stay out of trouble?

A: It stays on its best boo-havior.

Henry: Do zombies like sausage for breakfast?

Harry: No, they think it's the wurst.

Q: Why didn't Dracula sharpen his fangs?

A: He thought it was pointless.

Q: How do you wake up a chicken for Thanksgiving?

A: With an alarm cluck.

Q: Why can't ghosts fool anyone?

A: You can see right through them.

Q: What do you call a photo of a vampire's fangs?

A: A tooth pic

Q: Why did the farmer plant his phone in the garden?

A: He wanted to grow a call-iflower.

Q: Why did the preschoolers have to go to jail the day after Halloween?

A: They were kid-napping.

Q: Why did the farmer drop his tools on the ground?

A: He wanted to have a hoe-down.

Pete: Would a monster eat your math teacher?

Paul: You can count on it.

Q: **What do you get when you cross a mouse and a campfire on Halloween?**

A: A cheesy ghost story

Q: **Why did the witch put a frog in her drink?**

A: She wanted some croak-a-cola.

Q: **Who likes to sing about their Halloween candy?**

A: Candy rappers

Q: **Why couldn't Jimmy find a detective costume for Halloween?**

A: He was clueless.

Q: Why did the farmer want to be president?

A: So he could work for world peas.

Knock, knock.

Who's there?

Ears.

Ears who?

Ears a few more good Halloween jokes for you.

Q: What do you call a safe driver on Halloween?

A: Wreck-less

Q: What do you call a zombie who's lost his eyeballs?

A: Unsightly

Q: Why did the zombie dislike the farmers' market?

A: Because there were no farmers for sale.

Q: Why did the werewolf need a flea collar?

A: It was itching to howl at the moon.

Q: What do you get when you cross a dinosaur, a basset hound, and gorilla?

A: Dog-zilla

Q: Why don't rabbits like spooky stories?

A: Because it makes the hare stand up on the backs of their necks.

Q: If April showers bring May flowers, what do May flowers bring?

A: Pilgrims.

Q: What do you get when you cross Dracula and a cell phone?

A: A bat-mobile

Q: What is a turkey's favorite dessert?

A: Cherry gobbler

Q: What is a ghost's favorite movie?

A: *Goon with the Wind*

- -

Knock, knock.

Who's there?

Weed.

Weed who?

Weed better go trick-or-treating soon.

Knock, knock.

Who's there?

Dozen.

Dozen who?

Dozen anyone ever open their door on

Halloween anymore?

Knock, knock.

Who's there?

Wade.

Wade who?

Wade a minute—I want to go trick-or-treating too!

Q: What kind of mail do famous werewolves get?

A: Fang mail

Q: What is a witch's favorite cereal?

A: C-hex

Q: What is a pumpkin's least favorite sport?

A: Squash

Knock, knock.

Who's there?

Fitness.

Fitness who?

I'm fitness whole pumpkin pie in my mouth!

Knock, knock.

Who's there?

Wool.

Wool who?

Wool you go trick-or-treating with me?

Q: What is a werewolf's favorite holiday?

A: Fangs-giving

**Q: Why did the turkey decide to play
   the drums?**

A: Because he already had the drumsticks.

Q: What did the vet give the sick black cat?

A: A purr-scription

Knock, knock.

Who's there?

Sherwood.

Sherwood who?

Sherwood be nice if you'd come to the Halloween party with me.

Josh: Did you hear the joke about the skeleton?

Jeff: No, I haven't.

Josh: That's too bad—it's pretty humerus.

Q: Why did the vampire visit the library?

A: He was looking for a good book to sink his teeth into!

Knock, knock.

Who's there?

Window.

Window who?

Window we go trick-or-treating?

Q: Why isn't Dracula's nose 12 inches long?

A: Because then it would be a foot.

Q: Why did the turkey strike out at the ball game?

A: He kept hitting fowl balls.

Q: What do pumpkins wear for Halloween?

A: A har-vest

Sammy: Why are you slicing up all the dinner rolls?

Stuart: Because the doctor told me to cut my carbs.

Knock, knock.

Who's there?

Turkey.

Turkey who?

No, turkeys say "gobble, gobble." Owls say "who."

Knock, knock.

Who's there?

Cauliflower.

Cauliflower who?

Cauliflower doesn't have a last name.

Q: How do you know when a turkey is on the line?

A: You'll hear the phone go *wing, wing*.

Knock, knock.

Who's there?

Mustache.

Mustache who?

I mustache you if you want to go trick-or-treating.

Q: What country do monsters come from?

A: The imagi-nation

Q: What do you get when you cross a witch with a wasp?

A: A spell-ing bee

Q: What do zombies like to eat for dinner?

A: Tomb-stone pizzas

Knock, knock.

Who's there?

Lava.

Lava who?

I lava the leaves in autumn!

Knock, knock.

Who's there?

Kenya.

Kenya who?

Kenya come to the Halloween party?

Q: What do ghosts do when they can't get their computer to work?

A: They re-boo-t it.

Knock, knock.

Who's there?

Woo.

Woo who?

You seem pretty excited about Halloween!

Q: How do you find a zombie's house?

A: Look for a dead-end street.

Knock, knock.

Who's there?

Owen.

Owen who?

You Owen me some more Halloween candy!

Q: What do you get if you wear antlers with your pirate costume?

A: A buck-aneer

Q: Why does Humpty Dumpty like autumn so much?

A: Because he always has a great fall!

Q: Why did the vampire stop working?

A: Because he was on his coffin break.

Q: Why did the turkey have to go to the principal's office?

A: Because it was using fowl language.

Q: How do you know that someone has eaten too much on Thanksgiving?

A: Because they're thank-full.

Knock, knock.

Who's there?

Canoe.

Canoe who?

Canoe come over for Thanksgiving?

Knock, knock.

Who's there?

Yugo.

Yugo who?

Yugo trick-or-treat first, and I'll go second.

Knock, knock.

Who's there?

Howard.

Howard who?

Howard I know? He's wearing a Halloween costume!

Knock, knock.

Who's there?

Dora.

Dora who?

The Dora's locked on Halloween? That's crazy!

Q: Why did the girl put her Halloween candy under her pillow?

A: Because she wanted to have sweet dreams.

Knock, knock.

Who's there?

Juneau.

Juneau who?

Juneau, I think it's going to be a really great Halloween!

Knock, knock.

Who's there?

Gladys.

Gladys who?

I'm Gladys Halloween, because I love candy!

Q: What did the sweet potato say to the turkey?

A: "I yam what I yam!"

Knock, knock.

Who's there?

Cheryl.

Cheryl who?

I'm Cheryl get a lot of Halloween candy this year.

Q: What's blue and has feathers?

A: A turkey holding its breath

Q: What happens when you forget to put your turkey in the refrigerator?

A: It becomes fowl.

Q: What kind of key has feathers but can't open doors?

A: Tur-keys

Q: What do scarecrows and turkeys have in common?

A: They both get filled with stuffing.

Josh: Does Dracula like wearing plaid?

Jeff: I don't know, but I'll check.

Leah: Do you like corn for Thanksgiving?

Anna: It's a-maize-ing.

Q: When is a turkey funny?

A: When it's being a ham.

Knock, knock.

Who's there?

Witch.

Witch who?

I want to witch you a very Happy Halloween!

Q: Why didn't the mummy answer the phone?

A: Because he was tied up at the time.

Q: What's a werewolf's favorite time of year?

A: Howl-oween

Q: What did the goblin say to the skeleton?

A: "I've got a bone to pick with you!"

Q: Where do ghosts go to get training?

A: Boo-t camp

Knock, knock.

Who's there?

Who?

Who who?

Wouldn't you like to know!

Q: What did the leaf say to the tree?

A: I'm falling for you.

Knock, knock.

Who's there?

Twix.

Twix who?

Twix or treat.

Knock, knock.

Who's there?

Italy.

Italy who?

Italy a shame if you can't go trick-or-treating with us.

Knock, knock.

Who's there?

Darren.

Darren who?

I'm Darren you to wear a chicken costume for Halloween!

Knock, knock.

Who's there?

Owl.

Owl who?

Owl give you some of my Halloween candy if you open the door!

Knock, knock.

Who's there?

Donut.

Donut who?

Donut worry, be happy—it's Halloween!

Knock, knock.

Who's there?

Europe.

Europe who?

Europe to no good this Halloween, aren't you?

Knock, knock.

Who's there?

Gas.

Gas who?

Gas who has a great collection of Halloween jokes.

Q: What's a goblin's favorite food?

A: Ghoul-ash

Q: Why did the turkey want everyone to stay out of the kitchen?

A: Because it was dressing!

Q: How do pilgrims bake their pumpkin pies?

A: With May-flour

Q: What's it like to ride a witch's broom?

A: It's terri-flying.

Billy: You'll never be a pumpkin farmer.

Joey: Stop squashing my dreams!

Knock, knock.

Who's there?

Arthur.

Arthur who?

Arthur any leftovers from Thanksgiving dinner?

Knock, knock.

Who's there?

Idaho.

Idaho who?

Idaho the pumpkin patch, but I'm too busy trick-or-treating!

Knock, knock.

Who's there?

Lion.

Lion who?

I'd be lion if I said I didn't love Halloween!

Q: What do you get when you cross a zombie and a donut?

A: A hole-y terror

Q: What part of a turkey smells the best?

A: Its nose!

Q: What happens if you get sick on Halloween?

A: You get a fever and chills.

Q: What do you get when you cross a skeleton, a cyclops, and a piece of meat?

A: A rib-eye steak

Janie: How does that ghost look so young?

Jessie: It uses Boo-tox.

Q: When is it funny to be a farmer?

A: During the har-har-harvest

Q: What do you call a monster who's afraid of trick-or-treaters?

A: A Hallo-weenie

Q: What's an undertaker's favorite drink?

A: Cran-bury juice

Q: When is a turkey afraid to cross the road?

A: When he's a chicken.

Mom: Where are we going to put all the Thanksgiving leftovers?

Grandma: We'll cross that fridge when we come to it.

Q: Why do cyclopses get along so well?

A: They always see eye to eye.

Q: How often do you see a ghost?

A: Once in a boo moon

Q: What do you call it when a trick-or-treater gives you all his candy?

A: A blessing in disguise

Q: Why don't zombies eat elephants?

A: They don't want to bite off more than they can chew.

Q: What do scarecrows do when they're tired?

A: They hit the hay.

Stanley: Are you afraid of skeletons?

Henry: There's no bones about it.

Q: Why wouldn't Jimmy carve a pumpkin for Halloween?

A: He was out of his gourd.

Q: Why did the monster turn into a human?

A: Because you are what you eat.

Q: Who's the most fun at a Halloween party?

A: The owls—they're a hoot!

Q: Why can't you tell if it's a real ghost or a Halloween costume?

A: Because you can't judge a spook by its cover.

Q: How does everybody like the new cemetery?

A: It got grave reviews.

Knock, knock.

Who's there?

Radio.

Radio who?

Radio not, I'm going trick-or-treating!

Knock, knock.

Who's there?

Uganda.

Uganda who?

Uganda go trick-or-treating with me?

Knock, knock.

Who's there?

Jester.

Jester who?

Jester minute, I want to go to the Halloween party too!

Knock, knock.

Who's there?

Ketchup.

Ketchup who?

You better ketchup if you want to go trick-or-treating.

Q: How do you catch a ghost?

A: With a boo-by trap

Q: What do farmers say when they play poker?

A: "Weed 'em and reap!"

Betsy: What do you think of my egg costume?

Bailey: It cracks me up!

Q: Where do you put a crazy scarecrow?

A: In the funny farm

Q: What happened when the undertaker got a cramp in his leg?

A: He got a charley hearse.

Terry: Will zombies chew on your head?

Tommy: That's a no-brainer.

Q: What do you get when you cross a pig and a unicorn?

A: Pig-asus!

Q: What do you get when you cross Bigfoot and a pumpkin?

A: Sa-squash

Knock, knock.

Who's there?

Dragon.

Dragon who?

I'm tired of dragon this huge bag of Halloween candy.

Q: What do you get if you trick-or-treat at the train station?

A: Choo-choo-ing gum

Q: What happens if you lose track of time on Halloween?

A: You'll be choco-late for trick-or-treating!

Tongue Twisters—Say each one ten times fast!

Twisted turkey toes

Crunchy coated candy corn

Twitchy witches

Gross ghosts

Rare scarecrow

Knock, knock.

Who's there?

Oliver.

Oliver who?

I'm really sad this joke book is Oliver!

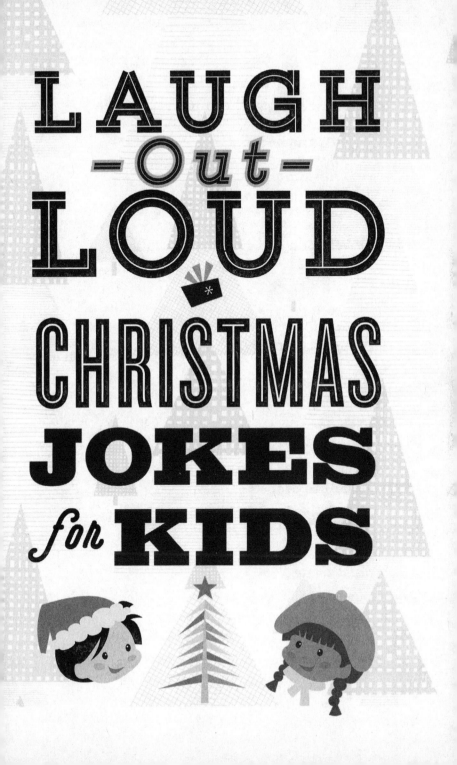

LAUGH
-Out-
LOUD

CHRISTMAS
JOKES
for KIDS

Q: What did the Christmas tree say to the ornament?

A: "Quit hanging around."

Q: What do snowmen eat for lunch?

A: Brrrr-itos

Q: Where does Santa keep his money?

A: In a snowbank

Q: What is a Christmas tree's least favorite month of the year?

A: Sep-timber

Q: What do you get when you mix a dog with a snowflake?

A: Frostbite

Q: Why did Santa feel bad about himself?

A: Because he had low elf-esteem.

Q: Why don't lobsters give Christmas presents?

A: Because they're shellfish.

Q: What do you call a cat who gives you presents?

A: Santa Paws

Q: What did Frosty wear to the wedding?

A: His snowsuit

Q: What is Jack Frost's favorite movie?

A: *The Blizzard of Oz*

Knock, knock.

Who's there?

Peas.

Peas who?

Peas tell me what you're giving me

for Christmas!

Knock, knock.

Who's there?

Norway.

Norway who?

There is Norway I'm kissing anybody

under the mistletoe!

Q: What is the coldest month of the year?

A: Decemb-rrrrr

Q: What is a tiger's favorite Christmas song?

A: "Jungle Bells"

Q: Why was Santa dressed up?

A: Because he was going to the snowball.

Q: Why do snowmen always change their minds?

A: Because they're flaky!

Q: Where do elves go to vote?

A: The North Poll

Q: Where does the Easter Bunny get his eggs at Christmastime?

A: From the three French hens

Q: What does Santa give Rudolph when he has bad breath?

A: Orna-mints

Q: What do snowmen wear on their feet?

A: Snowshoes

Knock, knock.

Who's there?

Freeze.

Freeze who?

Freeze a Jolly Good Fellow.

Q: Who brings Christmas presents to a shark?

A: Santa Jaws

Q: What's a polar bear's favorite cereal?

A: Ice Krispies

Knock, knock.

Who's there?

Hugo.

Hugo who?

Hugo sit on Santa's lap first, then I'll go second.

Knock, knock.

Who's there?

Dubai.

Dubai who?

I'm off Dubai some Christmas presents for you!

Knock, knock.

Who's there?

Butter.

Butter who?

You butter watch out. You butter not cry. You butter not pout I'm telling you why. . . .

Knock, knock.

Who's there?

Elf.

Elf who?

Elf finish wrapping the presents right away!

Q: What always falls at Christmas but never gets hurt?

A: Snow!

Santa: Elf, I have something to tell you.

Elf: I'm all ears.

Q: Why does Rudolph's nose shine at night?

A: Because he's a light sleeper.

Q: What did the gingerbread man do when he sprained his ankle?

A: He iced it.

Q: What do elves post on Facebook?

A: Elf-ies

Q: What do gingerbread men do before they go to bed?

A: Change their cookie sheets

Q: How do frogs celebrate Christmas?

A: They kiss under the mistle-toad.

- -

**Q: How do snowmen carry their books
to school?**

A: In their snowpacks

**Q: What do grumpy sheep say during
the holidays?**

A: "Baa, baa, humbug."

Q: What is a sheep's favorite Christmas song?

A: "Fleece Navidad"

Knock, knock.

Who's there?

Canoe.

Canoe who?

**Canoe help me put
up the Christmas tree?**

Knock, knock.

Who's there?

Wooden shoe.

Wooden shoe who?

Wooden shoe like to know what you're getting for Christmas?

Knock, knock.

Who's there?

Waldo.

Waldo who?

Waldo we do to celebrate New Year's Eve?

Q: Why do elves go to school?

A: To learn the elf-abet

- -

Q: Why can't a Christmas tree learn to knit?

A: Because they always drop their needles.

Q: Why doesn't Santa let the elves use

his computer?

A: They always delete the Christmas cookies.

Q: What is Santa's favorite kind of sandwich?

A: Peanut butter and jolly

Q: What is a penguin's favorite kind of cereal?

A: Frosted Flakes

Q: Where do Santa's reindeer stop for coffee?

A: Star-bucks

Knock, knock.

Who's there?

Myrrh.

Myrrh who?

Myrrh Christmas and a Happy New Year!

Knock, knock.

Who's there?

Udder.

Udder who?

Udder the tree you'll find your present!

Q: What do fish sing at Christmastime?

A: Christmas corals

Q: **What do ducks like to eat at Christmas parties?**

A: Cheese and quackers

Knock, knock.

Who's there?

Ya.

Ya who?

Wow, ya really excited about Christmas!

Knock, knock.

Who's there?

Iva.

Iva who?

Iva bunch of decorations to put on the tree.

Knock, knock.

Who's there?

Avenue.

Avenue who?

Avenue started your Christmas shopping yet?

Knock, knock.

Who's there?

Cannoli.

Cannoli who?

I cannoli eat one more Christmas cookie!

Q: Why did Santa pay top dollar for a box of candy canes?

A: Because they were in MINT condition!

Q: What goes *ho, ho, ho, thump*?

A: Santa laughing his head off!

Q: What do you call a snowman who vacations in Florida?

A: A puddle

Knock, knock.

Who's there?

Snow.

Snow who?

I snow what Santa's bringing you for Christmas.

Knock, knock.

Who's there?

Snowman.

Snowman who?

Snowman has ever seen Santa's workshop at the North Pole.

Q: What do you get when you cross a pinecone and a polar bear?

A: A fur tree

Q: Why did the math teacher get sick after Christmas dinner?

A: He had too much pi.

Q: What is an elf's favorite part of school?

A: Snow-and-tell

Q: What do you get when you combine a Christmas tree and an iPod?

A: A pineapple

Knock, knock.

Who's there?

Whale.

Whale who?

Whale, I can't believe the holidays are almost here!

Q: What does an elf listen to on the radio?

A: Wrap music

Q: Why doesn't Santa hide presents in the closet?

A: He has Claus-trophobia.

Knock, knock.

Who's there?

Dexter.

Dexter who?

Dexter halls with boughs of holly!

Q: How do snowmen spend their Christmas vacations?

A: Chilling out

Knock, knock.

Who's there?

Arthur.

Arthur who?

Arthur any more Christmas presents to open?

Q: **What does Santa give his reindeer for a stomachache?**

A: Elk-a-Seltzer

Q: **What do gingerbread men use when they break their legs?**

A: Candy canes

Q: **What is green, white, and red all over?**

A: An elf with sunburn

Q: **Why didn't the rope get any presents?**

A: Because it was knotty.

Q: **What did Mrs. Claus say to Rudolph when he was grumpy?**

A: "You need to lighten up!"

Q: How much did Santa pay for his reindeer?

A: A few bucks

Q: Why did the gingerbread man go to the doctor?

A: He was feeling crumb-y!

Q: What is something you can throw during the holidays but never catch?

A: A Christmas party

Q: Why doesn't Santa ever have spare change?

A: Because he's Jolly Old St. Nickel-less.

Q: How does a polar bear write out his Christmas list?

A: With a pen-guin

Q: Why was the cat put on Santa's naughty list?

A: Because he was a cheat-ah.

Q: How did the orange get into the Christmas stocking?

A: It squeezed its way in!

Knock, knock.

Who's there?

Annie.

Annie who?

Annie-body want some Christmas cookies?

Q: Why was the cat afraid to climb the Christmas tree?

A: It was scared of the bark!

Q: Why did Santa carry a giant sponge while delivering presents in Florida?

A: He wanted to soak up the sun!

Q: Why did Santa have a clock in his sleigh?

A: He wanted to watch time fly.

Q: How did the pony break its Christmas present?

A: It wouldn't stop horsing around.

Q: Why did the baker give everybody free cookies for Christmas?

A: Because he had a lot of dough!

Knock, knock.

Who's there?

Donut.

Donut who?

I donut know how Santa gets down the chimney on Christmas Eve!

Knock, knock.

Who's there?

Justin.

Justin who?

You're Justin time for Christmas carols.

Knock, knock.

Who's there?

Willie.

Willie who?

Willie keep his New Year's resolution this year?

Knock, knock.

Who's there?

Oldest.

Oldest who?

Oldest Christmas shopping is giving me a headache!

Knock, knock.

Who's there?

Snow place.

Snow place who?

There's snow place like home.

Q: What does the Easter Bunny like to drink during the holidays?

A: Eggnog

Knock, knock.

> Who's there?

Nutella.

> Nutella who?

There's Nutella what Santa might bring for Christmas this year.

Rita: What time is it when a polar bear sits in your chair?

Adam: I'm not sure.

Rita: It's time to get a new chair.

Knock, knock.

> Who's there?

Water.

> Water who?

Water you doing for New Year's Eve?

Q: Why is Santa so good at gardening?

A: Because he likes to hoe, hoe, hoe.

Knock, knock.

Who's there?

Tibet.

Tibet who?

Go Tibet early tonight, because Santa is coming!

Q: What did the astronaut get for Christmas?

A: A launch box

Q: What is a skunk's favorite Christmas song?

A: "Jingle Smells"

Knock, knock.

Who's there?

Juicy.

Juicy who?

Juicy all the pretty Christmas lights?

Knock, knock.

Who's there?

Rabbit.

Rabbit who?

Rabbit up with paper and ribbon, and put it under the tree.

Q: What kind of motorcycle does Santa drive?

A: A Holly Davidson

Knock, knock.

Who's there?

Quiche.

Quiche who?

Quiche me under the mistletoe!

Knock, knock.

Who's there?

Jester.

Jester who?

In jester minute it'll be the New Year!

Q: What's a mermaid's favorite Christmas story?

A: *A Christmas Coral*

Q: What did the rattlesnakes do at their Christmas party?

A: They hissed under the mistletoe.

Q: What do elves use to wash their hands?

A: Santa-tizer

Q: What do you call it when people are afraid of Santa?

A: Claus-trophobic

Q: What do boxers like to drink at Christmas parties?

A: Punch!

Knock, knock.

Who's there?

Yule.

Yule who?

Yule really like your Christmas present this year.

Knock, knock.

Who's there?

Anna.

Anna who?

Anna partridge in a pear tree.

Q: How did the crab wish his mom a Merry Christmas?

A: He called her on his shell phone.

Q: Why does a cat take so long to wrap Christmas presents?

A: He won't stop until they're purr-fect.

Q: Why did Santa go buy more reindeer?

A: They were on sale and didn't cost much doe!

Q: Why did the elf have to stay after school?

A: He was in trouble for losing his gnome-work.

Knock, knock.

Who's there?

Roach.

Roach who?

I roach you a letter to wish you Merry Christmas!

Q: How does Frosty get around?

A: On his ice-cycle

Q: What do pigs use to write their Christmas list for Santa?

A: A pig pen

Q: How do elves learn to chop down a Christmas tree?

A: They go to boarding school.

Q: Why did the Christmas tree go to bed early?

A: It was bushed!

Q: What does Frosty do when he feels stressed out?

A: He takes a chill pill.

Q: Why was the chicken put on Santa's naughty list?

A: It kept laying deviled eggs.

Q: What do you get when you cross a lobster and Santa?

A: Santa Claws

Knock, knock.

Who's there?

Arthur.

Arthur who?

My Arthur-ritis is acting up from the winter weather.

Q: What is Santa's favorite singer?

A: Elf-is Presley

Knock, knock.

Who's there?

Wart.

Wart who?

Wart is your favorite Christmas carol?

Q: What do you call a snowman's kids?

A: Chilled-ren

Q: What did the one penguin say to the other?

A: "Ice to meet you."

Q: What's a dinosaur's least favorite reindeer?

A: Comet

Q: What do polar bears wear on their heads?

A: Snowcaps

Q: What do penguins use in science class?

A: Beak-ers

Q: What did the candy cane say to the ornament?

A: "Hang in there."

Q: What do you call it when the elves take a break?

A: A Santa pause

George: Whose music is best for decking the halls?

James: A-wreath-a Franklin's!

Q: How does the alphabet change during the holidays?

A: The Christmas alphabet has noel.

Knock, knock.

Who's there?

Owl.

Owl who?

Owl always love to celebrate Christmas.

Q: What is Santa Claus's nationality?

A: North Polish

Knock, knock.

Who's there?

Alba.

Alba who?

Alba home for Christmas.

Knock, knock.

Who's there?

Wayne.

Wayne who?

A Wayne a manger.

Josh: Do you know how much Santa paid for his sleigh and reindeer?

Jeff: Maybe a few bucks?

Josh: Nothing! It was on the house.

Q: What do you call a polar bear in the Caribbean?

A: Lost!

Q: What did the chicken have to do after eating all the Christmas cookies?

A: Egg-cercise

Knock, knock.

Who's there?

Uno.

Uno who?

Uno Christmas is a season for giving.

Knock, knock.

Who's there?

Latte.

Latte who?

Thanks a latte for all the Christmas presents!

Q: What kind of cookies make Santa laugh?

A: Snickerdoodles

Q: Why wouldn't Rudolph stay in the barn?

A: Because he was un-stable.

Q: What's an elf's favorite Christmas song?

A: "I'll Be Gnome for Christmas"

Q: What does a whale write in his Christmas cards?

A: Sea-sons greetings!

Knock, knock.

Who's there?

Turnip.

Turnip who?

Turnip the Christmas music!

Q: What does Santa wear when he goes golfing?

A: A tee-shirt

Knock, knock.

Who's there?

Dishes.

Dishes who?

Dishes going to be the best Christmas we've ever had.

Q: How did the turtle behave at the Christmas party?

A: He wouldn't come out of his shell.

Knock, knock.

Who's there?

Interrupting Santa.

Interrupting San—

Ho, ho, ho!

Q: How do you know Santa is good at karate?

A: Because he wears a black belt.

Knock, knock.

Who's there?

Pasture.

Pasture who?

Pasture eggnog—I'm thirsty!

**Q: Which one of Santa's reindeer likes to clean
the workshop?**

A: Comet

Q: **How did Santa feel when his reindeer got fleas?**

A: It really ticked him off!

Q: **What do you have in December that's not in any other month?**

A: The letter *D*

Q: **What's a mime's favorite Christmas carol?**

A: "Silent Night"

Q: **What do snowmen say when they play hide-and-seek?**

A: "I-cy you!"

Q: **What do polar bears put on their tacos?**

A: Chilly sauce

Q: Why does Santa go down the chimney?

A: Because it soots him.

Q: Why does a broken drum make a great Christmas present?

A: Because you just can't beat it!

Q: Who does Frosty like to visit during the holidays?

A: His aunt Arctica

Q: What's a polar bear's favorite dinner?

A: Ham-brrrrr-gers

Tongue Twisters

Crispy Christmas cookies

Twelve twisted elves

Santa's snowy sleigh

Plump penguins

Q: Where do skunks like to sit during Christmas church service?

A: In the front pew

Q: What do you get when you cross a dinosaur and an evergreen?

A: A tree rex

Q: Why were Santa's reindeer so itchy?

A: From the antarc-ticks

Knock, knock.

Who's there?

Watson.

Watson who?

Watson your Christmas wish list this year?

Knock, knock.

Who's there?

Yoda.

Yoda who?

Yoda one I want to wish a Merry Christmas!

Knock, knock.

Who's there?

Soda.

Soda who?

It's soda-pressing that the holidays are almost over!

Q: What did one iceberg say to the other?

A: "I think we're drifting apart."

Knock, knock.

Who's there?

Ivy.

Ivy who?

Ivy lot of Christmas cards to put in the mail!

Q: How do snowmen like their root beer?

A: In a frosted mug

Q: What did the basil say to the oregano?

A: "Seasoning's greetings."

Q: Why couldn't Jack Frost go

Christmas shopping?

A: Because his bank account was frozen!

Sam: Did you have fun at the pig's Christmas party?

Sue: No, it was a boar.

Knock, knock.

Who's there?

Brett.

Brett who?

I Brett you don't know what's in your Christmas stocking!

Q: What do you get when you cross Santa Claus and the Easter Bunny?

A: Jolly beans

Q: How did Humpty Dumpty feel after he finished Christmas shopping?

A: Eggs-hausted

Q: Why did Rudolph put his money in the freezer?

A: He wanted some cold, hard cash!

Q: Where do crocodiles keep their eggnog?

A: In the refriger-gator

Knock, knock.

Who's there?

Otter.

Otter who?

You otter come to my house for Christmas this year.

Q: Why was the owl so popular at the Christmas party?

A: He was a hoot!

Q: How do reindeer carry their oats?

A: In a buck-et

Knock, knock.

Who's there?

Nacho.

Nacho who?

It's nacho turn to open a Christmas present.

Q: Why won't snowmen eat any carrot cake?

A: They're afraid it has boogers in it.

Q: What do you get when you combine Santa Claus and Sherlock Holmes?

A: Santa Clues

Q: How do Santa's reindeer know when it's time to deliver presents?

A: They check their calen-deer.

Q: Why do fishermen send Santa so many letters?

A: They love dropping him a line.

Knock, knock.

Who's there?

Bacon.

Bacon who?

I'm bacon dozens of Christmas cookies this year!

Q: Why didn't the beetle like Christmas?

A: Because he was a humbug.

Q: What is Santa's favorite kind of candy?

A: Jolly Ranchers

Q: Why did Frosty get kicked out of the farmer's market?

A: He was caught picking his nose.

Q: Why wouldn't the turkey eat dessert after Christmas dinner?

A: He was too stuffed.

Q: Where do bugs like to shop for their Christmas presents?

A: At the flea market

Q: Why doesn't Santa ever worry about the past?

A: Because he's always focused on the present.

Q: What's the best state for listening to Christmas music?

A: South Carol-ina

Q: What kind of animal needs an umbrella?

A: Rain-deer

Q: What happened when Santa took a nap in the fireplace?

A: He slept like a log.

Knock, knock.

Who's there?

Acid.

Acid who?

Acid I'd stop by and bring you a Christmas present.

Q: What do you call decorations hanging from Rudolph's antlers?

A: Christmas horn-aments

Q: Why did the snowman's mouth hurt?

A: Because he had a coal sore.

Q: What do polar bears eat for lunch?

A: Iceberg-ers

Knock, knock.

Who's there?

Walnut.

Walnut who?

I walnut let the holidays go by without wishing you a Merry Christmas!

Knock, knock.

Who's there?

Muffin.

Muffin who?

Naughty kids get muffin for Christmas.

Q: Where do people sing Christmas songs quietly?

A: Bethle-hum

Q: How do you find your way to the New Year's Eve party?

A: Follow the auld lang signs.

Knock, knock.

Who's there?

Les.

Les who?

Les go caroling and get some hot chocolate!

Q: What happened when the dentist didn't get a Christmas present?

A: It really hurt his fillings.

Knock, knock.

Who's there?

Mustache.

Mustache who?

I mustache you to come to my Christmas party!

Q: What do you get when you combine a penguin and a jalapeño?

A: A chilly pepper

Knock, knock.

Who's there?

Meow.

Meow who?

Meow-y Christmas!

Q: How do you decorate a scientist's lab for Christmas?

A: With a chemis-tree

Knock, knock.

Who's there?

Dachshund.

Dachshund who?

Dachshund through the snow in a one-horse open sleigh.

Q: What shoes did the baker wear while baking holiday bread?

A: His loafers

Q: What kinds of trees wear gloves in the winter?

A: Palm trees

Q: Why don't you want to make a
snowman angry?

A: He might have a total meltdown.

Knock, knock.

Who's there?

Dragon.

Dragon who?

I'm dragon my feet on getting my Christmas
shopping done.

Q: Who watched out for the snowman during
the blizzard?

A: His snow angel

Q: Why did the mom put her son in the corner
after he went snowboarding?

A: She wanted him to warm up in 90 degrees.

Knock, knock.

Who's there?

Cole.

Cole who?

Cole goes in naughty kids' stockings.

Q: Why would you invite a mushroom to a Christmas party?

A: Because he's a fungi.

Q: What do you call a dentist who cleans the abominable snowman's teeth?

A: CRAZY!!!

Q: What do Halloween mummies and Christmas elves have in common?

A: They both have a lot of wrapping.

- -

Q: What kind of drink is never ready on time?

A: Hot choco-late

Knock, knock.

Who's there?

Butcher.

Butcher who?

Butcher arms around me and give me a kiss under the mistletoe.

Q: Why don't polar bears and penguins get along?

A: Because they're polar opposites.

Q: What do you call a cow that lives in an igloo?

A: An Eski-moo

Q: What do you call Frosty's cell phone?

A: A snow-mobile

Q: What do you give a baboon for Christmas?

A: A monkey wrench

Q: What do you give a wasp for Christmas?

A: A bee-bee gun

Q: What do squirrels have for breakfast on Christmas morning?

A: Do-nuts

Q: What did the whale get in its Christmas stocking?

A: Blubber gum

Q: What do you get when Jack Frost turns on the radio?

A: Really cool music

Q: Why didn't the cow like its crummy Christmas present?

A: It was a milk dud.

Q: How do starfish celebrate the holiday season?

A: With yule-tide greetings

Knock, knock.

Who's there?

Hailey.

Hailey who?

I'm Hailey a cab so we'll make it to the Christmas party on time!

Q: What do you give a lamb for Christmas?

A: A sheeping bag

Knock, knock.

Who's there?

Howie.

Howie who?

Howie going to get that big star on top of the Christmas tree?

Knock, knock.

Who's there?

Noah.

Noah who?

Noah good place to buy candy canes?

Knock, knock.

Who's there?

Taco.

Taco who?

Let's taco 'bout what we'll do for

Christmas vacation!

Knock, knock.

Who's there?

Dawn.

Dawn who?

Dawn forget to leave cookies for Santa on Christmas Eve!

Knock, knock.

Who's there?

Betty.

Betty who?

I Betty can't guess what I got him for Christmas!

Knock, knock.

Who's there?

Cold.

Cold who?

Cold you come out and build a snowman with me?

195

Q: What happened to Santa when he went down the chimney?

A: He got the flue.

Q: What do you get from a cow that receives too many presents for Christmas?

A: Spoiled milk!

Knock, knock.

Who's there?

Luke.

Luke who?

Luke up in the sky for Santa's sleigh!

Knock, knock.

Who's there?

Howard.

Howard who?

Howard you like to make some

Christmas cookies?

Q: How did the mad scientist cause a blizzard?

A: He was brainstorming.

Jimmy: What do you call a wreath under a pile

of snow?

Joey: A holly bury

Q: Why did the librarian have to miss the

Christmas party?

A: She was double-booked.

Q: Why did the polar bear get glasses?

A: To improve its ice-sight (eyesight)

Q: How does an Eskimo fix his broken sled?

A: With i-glue

Q: Why did Santa sing lullabies to his sack?

A: He wanted a sleeping bag.

Q: Why did Rudolph need braces?

A: Because he had buck teeth.

Q: Why did Santa use Rudolph to guide his sleigh?

A: It was a bright idea.

Q: What did one Christmas light say to the other?

A: "Do you want to go out tonight?"

Q: Why was Mrs. Claus crying?

A: She stubbed her mistletoe.

Q: Why is the Grinch so good at gardening?

A: He has a green thumb.

Q: Why was the frosting so stressed out?

A: It was spread too thin.

Q: Why wouldn't the parakeet buy his girlfriend a Christmas present?

A: Because he was cheep.

Q: Why are pigs so fun at Christmas parties?

A: Because they go hog wild.

Q: What do you call a guy whose snowmobile breaks down?

A: A cab

Q: Why don't you invite the Polar Express to dinner?

A: It always choo-choos with its mouth open.

Knock, knock.

Who's there?

Raymond.

Raymond who?

Raymond me to leave out some cookies

for Santa.

Knock, knock.

Who's there?

Johanna.

Johanna who?

Johanna come out and build a snowman?

Knock, knock.

Who's there?

Duncan.

Duncan who?

Duncan cookies in hot cocoa is delicious!

Q: Why wasn't a creature stirring on Christmas Eve?

A: Because they had already finished making their Christmas soup.

Joe: Did your goat eat my hat and mittens?

Jim: Yes, he scarfed them right down.

Q: What's as big as a polar bear but weighs nothing?

A: A polar bear's shadow

Q: Why wouldn't Rudolph leave the barn to guide the sleigh?

A: He was stalling.

Q: **What do porcupines say when they kiss under the mistletoe?**

A: "Ouch!"

Q: **What happened when the frog's snowmobile broke down?**

A: It had to be toad away.

Q: **What did Mrs. Claus say when Santa came home late?**

A: "Where on earth have you been?"

Q: **What did the fish think of its Christmas present?**

A: She thought it was fin-tastic!

Q: What did Santa say when Mrs. Claus made him coffee?

A: "Thanks a latte!"

Q: What do you get when you cross a duck and a squirrel?

A: A nut-quacker

Q: What do you get when you cross a reindeer and a fish?

A: Ru-dolphin

Q: Why was the skunk put on Santa's naughty list?

A: Because he was a stinker.

Jack: Why did you give me worms for Christmas?

Jeff: Because they were dirt cheap!

Q: What do you do if a polar bear is in your bed?

A: Find a hotel for the night!

Q: What do you get if you cross a turtle and a snowman?

A: A snow-poke

Q: What did the Dalmatian say after Christmas dinner?

A: "That hit the spot!"

Q: How do you feel after drinking hot cocoa?

A: Marsh-mellow

Q: How do you know if there's a polar bear in your refrigerator?

A: The door won't close!

Q: How do alligators cook their Christmas dinner?

A: In a croc-pot

Q: What do you get when you cross a pine tree with a hyena?

A: An ever-grin tree

Q: What do you get if you put your head in the punch bowl?

A: Egg-noggin

- -

Q: What's the best thing to drink on Christmas Eve?

A: Nativi-tea

Q: What do you get when you cross a squirrel and a Christmas pirate?

A: Treasure chestnuts roasting on an open fire

Q: What do you get when an astronaut goes skiing?

A: An ava-launch

Q: What did one skier say to the other skier?

A: "It's all downhill from here."

Q: What's Santa's favorite book?

A: *Merry Poppins*

Q: What kind of dinosaur hibernates for the winter?

A: A bronto-snore-us

Q: Why did the child need new glasses for Christmas?

A: He didn't have visions of sugarplums dancing in his head.

Q: What do reindeer have that no other animals have?

A: Baby reindeer

Q: Did you hear about the cat who chewed on the Christmas lights?

A: It was shocking!

Q: Did you hear about the Christmas star?

A: It's out of this world.

Q: Why couldn't the fish go Christmas shopping?

A: It didn't have anemone.

Q: How do you spell *frozen* with only three letters?

A: *I-C-E!*

Q: What kind of snowmobile does a farmer like to ride?

A: A Cow-asaki

Q: How does a grizzly get through the holidays?

A: He grins and bears it.

Q: How did the wise men sneak across the desert?

A: They had camel-flage.

Q: What do you get when a polar bear sits on a pumpkin?

A: Squash

Q: How do you pay when you're Christmas shopping?

A: With jingle bills

Q: What kind of toy does a chicken want for Christmas?

A: A Jack-in-the-bok-bok-box!

Q: How does an opera singer make Christmas cookies?

A: With icing (I sing)

Brother: I broke my candy cane in two places.

Sister: Then don't go to those places anymore!

Julie: Did you have fun at the Christmas party?

Josie: No, it was a Feliz Navi-dud.

Q: How do you invite a fish to your Christmas party?

A: Drop it a line.

Q: What did Santa say when he parked his sleigh?

A: "There's snow place like home."

Q: Why did the snowman need dandruff shampoo?

A: Because he had snowflakes.

Knock, knock.

Who's there?

Window.

Window who?

Window you want to open your Christmas presents?

Q: Why did the girl give the boy an orange for Christmas?

A: Because he was her main squeeze.

Q: What do you get when you hang a turkey from the fireplace?

A: A stocking stuffer

Q: Why did the girl get celery for Christmas?

A: It was a stalk-ing stuffer.

Knock, knock.

Who's there?

Don.

Don who?

Don you want to come out and play in the snow?

Knock, knock.

Who's there?

Sarah.

Sarah who?

Sarah reason you're not having any Christmas cookies?

Knock, knock.

Who's there?

Funnel.

Funnel who?

The funnel start once everyone shows up to the party!

Brother: Is this present from Mom?

Sister: Ap-parent-ly it is!

Q: What's a cow's favorite Christmas song?

A: "Jingle Bulls"

Q: What is an elf's favorite dessert?

A: Shortbread cookies

Knock, knock.

Who's there?

Braydon.

Braydon who?

Are you Braydon your hair for the Christmas party?

Q: How does Santa get into his chalet?

A: With a s-key (ski)

Q: What do you put in a hyena's Christmas stocking?

A: A Snickers bar

Q: Why was the snowman so mean?

A: Because he was coldhearted.

Q: What do you get when you mix Rudolph and the queen?

A: A reign-deer

Knock, knock.

Who's there?

Police.

Police who?

Police come over for Christmas dinner!

Knock, knock.

Who's there?

Ice cream.

Ice cream who?

Ice cream when I see the abominable snowman!

Q: **What do you get when you combine a snowball, a fish, and a Christmas tree branch?**

A: A frozen fish stick

Knock, knock.

Who's there?

Megan.

Megan who?

It's Megan me crazy having to wait to open my presents!

Knock, knock.

Who's there?

Glove.

Glove who?

I glove the holidays.

Q: Why does Santa like his sleigh?

A: Because it's satis-flying.

Q: Why do reindeer eat so many candy canes?

A: For nourish-mint

Q: Why did the snowman get a headache?

A: He had brain freeze.

Q: Why did Santa's reindeer go to jail?

A: For Comet-ting a crime

Q: What kind of dogs saw the Christmas star?

A: German shepherds

Q: Why couldn't the conductor drive the Polar Express?

A: He didn't have enough training.

Q: How do pirates save money on their Christmas shopping?

A: They look for sails.

Q: Why did Santa go back for more dessert?

A: Because he wanted to retreat.

Q: How does a sailor get to church on Christmas Eve?

A: On his wor-ship

Tongue Twisters

Round red wreath.

Striped stuffed stockings.

Green glitter glue.

Santa sings silly sleigh songs.

Q: Why did the dog always get depressed at Christmas?

A: Because the holidays were ruff.

Cassie: Did the cow like the present you got him?

Kendra: No, he thought it was udderly ridiculous.

- -

Knock, knock.

Who's there?

Ville.

Ville who?

No, the opposite: it's Whoville.

Knock, knock.

Who's there?

Hammond.

Hammond who?

Hammond eggs taste great on

Christmas morning.

Q: Why was the farmer on Santa's naughty list?

A: Because his pig squealed on him!

Q: What do you call a twig that doesn't like Christmas?

A: A stick-in-the-mud

Q: How did the turkey get home for Christmas?

A: In a gravy boat

Q: Why do baseball players love Christmas dinner?

A: They like to be behind the plate.

Q: What is a squirrel's favorite part of the Christmas season?

A: Going to see *The Nutcracker*

Billy: I got my pig some soap for Christmas.

Ben: That's hogwash!

Knock, knock.

Who's there?

Lion.

Lion who?

I'd be lion if I told you I didn't love the holidays.

Q: How do you make a strawberry shake?

A: Introduce it to the abominable snowman.

Knock, knock.

Who's there?

Weed.

Weed who?

Weed better leave for the Christmas party or we'll be late!

Knock, knock.

Who's there?

Kenya.

Kenya who?

Kenya tell me your favorite Christmas tradition?

Q: Why did the moon get sick after eating Christmas dinner?

A: Because it was so full.

Q: Which baseball player makes the best Christmas cakes?

A: The batter

Q: How do the Christmas angels greet each other?

A: They say, "Halo."

Q: What happened when the rabbit ate too many Christmas cookies?

A: It was hopped up on sugar.

Q: Why don't crabs spend much money for Christmas?

A: Because they're penny-pinchers.

Q: Why don't hyenas get sick in the winter?

A: Because laughter is the best medicine.

Sally: What if Jimmy can't play the trumpet in the Christmas concert?

Suzie: We'll find a substi-toot.

Q: Why did the boy hang triangles on his Christmas tree?

A: So he could have a geome-tree.

Q: What do reindeer like to eat with their spaghetti?

A: Meat-bells

Luke: Does Santa like to study chemistry?

Stew: Only periodically.

Knock, knock.

Who's there?

Dozen.

Dozen who?

Dozen anyone want to sing a Christmas carol?

Knock, knock.

Who's there?

Reindeer.

Reindeer who?

It's going to reindeer, so you'd better bring an umbrella.

Q: Why do hummingbirds hum

Christmas carols?

A: Because they can't remember the words.

Q: How do ducks celebrate New Year's Eve?

A: With fire-quackers

Q: What is something that's easy to catch in the

winter, but hard to throw?

A: A cold

Q: Why did the raisin stay home from the

Christmas party?

A: Because it couldn't find a date.

Knock, knock.

Who's there?

Orange.

Orange who?

Orange you glad Christmas is almost here?

Q: What kind of fruit decorates a Christmas tree?

A: A pineapple

Q: Why did the orange stop Christmas shopping?

A: Because it ran out of juice.

Q: What do you get when your dog plays too long in the snow?

A: A pup-sicle

Knock, knock.

Who's there?

Candice.

Candice who?

Candice holiday season get any better?

Knock, knock.

Who's there?

Juan.

Juan who?

Juan a kiss under the mistletoe?

Knock, knock.

Who's there?

Minnow.

Minnow who?

Let minnow if you can't make it to the Christmas party.

Q: What happened when the cucumber ran out of wrapping paper?

A: It left him in a pickle.

Susie: Is your Christmas gift here yet?

Sally: Yes, it's present.

Caleb: Do you like the red frosting on my Christmas cookies?

Callie: Yes, it's to dye for.

Q: What does Santa use for a map?

A: A snow globe

Q: Why do kids get bad grades during the holidays?

A: Because it's D-cember.

Q: What did Santa say when the elf told a funny joke?

A: "You sleigh me!"

Q: What do you give a rabbit for Christmas?

A: A hare-brush

Q: What do you give a flea for Christmas?

A: An Itch A Sketch

Q: Why did the boy get a bucket for Christmas?

A: Because he looked a little pail.

Stanley: Did your dad like the statue you gave him for Christmas?

Henry: No, it was a bust.

Eva: Did you know Santa's suit is exactly the right size?

Ava: Well, that's fitting.

Q: Why do snowmen wear sunglasses?

A: To keep the sun out of their ice.

Anna: Should we get Dad a drill for Christmas?

Ella: No, that's boring.

Q: Why is Christmas so exciting?

A: Because it's an advent-ure.

Q: Why won't Santa wear an itchy scarf?

A: Because it's a pain in the neck.

Q: How did Santa feel about the house with the security system?

A: He was alarmed!

Q: Where did Noah like to go in the winter?

A: All the way to the ark-tic

Q: How does Santa know what to give a zebra for Christmas?

A: The answer is black and white.

Josie: You forgot the lamb for the nativity scene!

Jamie: Well, I feel sheepish.

Q: Why can't Martians get along at Christmas?

A: Because they're alienated from one another.

Q: When is it hard to hear a Christmas movie?

A: When it's ani-muted

Q: How did Santa feel when he got soot on his suit?

A: He felt ash-amed.

Lucy: Are you allowed to make up a Christmas story?

Lena: Yes, I'm authorized.

Q: What does a ghost think about Christmas carols?

A: It thinks they're boo-tiful.

Q: How does a wolf like its Christmas cookies?

A: Bite-sized.

Tory: Why did Santa put tuna in my stocking?

Terry: He thought it would be bene-fish-ial.

Q: Why do elves like to go camping?

A: Because they're so compe-tent.

Q: Why don't we go camping in the winter?

A: Because it's too in-tents.

Q: How do you know when a snowman doesn't like you?

A: He'll give you the cold shoulder.

Jane: My mom won't let me embroider my Christmas stocking!

Jill: Well, that's crewel!

Q: Why did Mrs. Claus give Rudolph a hug?

A: Because he was so deer.

Q: Why was the beaver so sad at Christmas?

A: Because his present was dam-aged.

Q: Why did the elf have to clean up after the reindeer?

A: Because it was his doody.

Q: Why do cows like to sing Christmas carols?

A: Because they're so moo-sical.

Q: Why do elves always wear perfume?

A: They think it's e-scent-ial.

Q: **What did Luke Skywalker say at Christmas dinner?**

A: "May the fork be with you."

Q: **Why did Santa fly his sleigh through the Grand Canyon?**

A: He thought it was gorge-ous.

Q: **When does sledding make you laugh?**

A: When it's hill-arious

Q: **How do cows pay for their Christmas shopping?**

A: With their moo-lah

Q: When can't you put any jelly in your stocking?

A: When it's already jam-packed.

Q: Why shouldn't the reindeer make fun of Rudolph's nose?

A: Because it's impo-light.

Darla: When should we sing Christmas carols?

Debby: Hymn-ediately!

Q: Why is Santa so jolly?

A: Because he's a good fellow.

Q: Which size cup of hot cocoa tastes the best?

A: A medi-yum

Mrs. Claus: I ironed your Santa suit for Christmas Eve.

Santa: I'm impressed!

Q: Why was the chef late for Christmas dinner?

A: He ran out of thyme.

Q: What do you call a great snowplow driver?

A: Wreckless

Q: What happens if you see a polar bear at the shopping center?

A: You might get mall-ed.

Q: How do you see an ice-cream cone from far away?

A: Use a tele-scoop.

Q: What does a hen have for dessert at Christmas?

A: Layer cake

Q: How did the wise men know to follow the star?

A: They had frankin-sense.

Q: How do you make your Christmas cards unique?

A: You put your own stamp on them.

Q: Why were the reindeer mad at Santa?

A: He drove them up the wall.

Q: Why did two skunks give each other the same present?

A: Because great minds stink alike.

Q: Does Santa worry about delivering all the presents?

A: No, he's got it in the bag.

Q: How did the Three Little Pigs stay merry at Christmas?

A: They kept their chinny-chin-chins up.

Q: When does Santa deliver presents to the sheep?

A: Last but not fleeced

Kelly: Will Santa bring my dog a present?

Karly: Make no bones about it.

Q: What did Santa say to the naughty squirrel?

A: "If you can't say something nice, don't say nuttin' at all."

Q: How did the canary afford all her Christmas gifts?

A: She used her nest egg.

Curtis: Are you excited to put up the
Christmas tree?

Carter: Yes, I'm on pines and needles!

Gary: Is this star too fancy for our
Christmas tree?

Mary: Yes, I think it's over-the-top.

Q: Why doesn't Blitzen ever get in trouble?

A: He's always passing the buck.

Q: Why is everyone happy at the North Pole?

A: Because they're on top of the world.

**Q: Why does Santa keep a hammer in his sleigh
on Christmas Eve?**

A: So he can beat the clock.

Q: When will Santa come down the chimney?

A: In the Nick of time

Q: When should you open your Christmas gifts?

A: There's no time like the present.

Q: Why won't you ever see the gingerbread man cry?

A: Because he's one tough cookie.

Bobby: Santa makes you mad?

Billy: Yes, every time he's here I see red.

Q: Why did the mittens get married?

A: It was glove at first sight.

Q: When do you bring lipstick under

the mistletoe?

A: If you want to kiss and makeup.

Q: Why did the elf bring his garbage on a date

to the movies?

A: He wanted to take out the trash.

Q: Where do you keep your Santa suit?

A: In the Santa Claus-et

Q: When does a weatherman need an umbrella?

A: When his Christmas cookies have sprinkles

Q: Why did Santa hire an elephant for his workshop?

A: Because it would work for peanuts.

Q: How does a chicken get to the Christmas party?

A: In a heli-coop-ter

Q: Why did the pig look great at the Christmas party?

A: Because it was so sty-lish.

Q: How is a wool cardigan like a guy at the gym?

A: They're both heavy sweaters.

Q: Are the reindeer excited about the Christmas party?

A: Yes, they'll be there with bells on.

Grandma: Did Jimmy like the soccer ball I gave him for Christmas?

Grandpa: He got a kick out of it.

Q: What do sharks eat for Christmas dessert?

A: Octo-pie

Ralphie: Why did you give me lettuce for Christmas?

Alfie: You said you wanted to get ahead.

Q: How did Dorothy know what to give the Scarecrow for Christmas?

A: It was a no-brainer.

Q: Why did the boy keep asking for a train for Christmas?

A: He had a one-track mind.

Q: What did the alien think about his Christmas present?

A: He thought it was out of this world.

Q: What do polar bears want for breakfast on Christmas morning?

A: Grrrr-nola

Q: What do you get when you cross a reindeer and a ghost?

A: A cari-boo

Knock, knock.

Who's there?

Alpine.

Alpine who?

Alpine trees look great with Christmas lights.

Q: What did the pirate say when he was freezing in the snow?

A: "Shiver me timbers!"

Q: What game do you give a mouse for Christmas?

A: Par-cheesy

Q: Why can't ponies sing Christmas carols?

A: Because they're a little horse.

Toby: I ruined the treats for Christmas.

Tommy: Oh, fudge!

Q: When is a puppy like a cold winter's day?

A: When it's nippy

Q: Why did the Easter Bunny go trick-or-treating at Christmas?

A: He was in a holi-daze.

Q: Why would you give away a fireplace for free?

A: You must have a big hearth.

Q: What happens if you give a snowman a carrot?

A: He'll get nosy.

Q: Why won't penguins use cell phones?

A: Because they're cold-fashioned.

Q: What do you call Santa when his suit is wrinkled?

A: Kris Krinkle

Sara: Why won't your parents eat almonds at Christmastime?

Dora: They're nuts.

Q: What will happen if you run out of peppermints?

A: People will raise cane!

Q: Why was Santa sad?

A: He didn't think his parents believed in him.

Q: Why couldn't Rudolph buy any more soap?

A: He was all washed-up.

Q: What did the snowplow driver say at the end of the season?

A: "It was nice snowing you."

Q: What's a turkey's favorite Christmas dessert?

A: Bluberry gobbler

Q: Why couldn't the elf pay for her Christmas shopping?

A: She was a little short.

Q: What happened when the reindeer flew into a mountain?

A: They couldn't get over it.

Knock, knock.

Who's there?

Alpaca.

Alpaca who?

Alpaca bag and visit Grandma for Christmas.

Q: Why shouldn't you do homework while you're ice-skating?

A: Your grades might slip.

Jeremy: Why do you believe in Santa Claus?

Jillian: Because the Easter Bunny and the tooth fairy told me he's real.

Q: What did the rabbit say to the frog?

A: "Hoppy Holidays!"

Wyatt: Did you hear we're just

having sandwiches for Christmas dinner?

William: That's a bunch of baloney!

Q: What does a frog say when it's unwrapping

its Christmas presents?

A: "Rip it, rip it, rip it."

Q: Why wouldn't the skeleton go snowboarding

down the mountain?

A: He didn't have the guts.

Olivia: Did you know lots of reindeer live in Alaska?

Violet: That's what I herd.

Aunt Sue: Is Alex disappointed that he caught a cold at Christmas?

Uncle Sam: He'll get over it.

Bess: Do you like the trampoline Santa gave you for Christmas?

Tess: I'm jumping for joy!

Q: Why was the dog barking at the fireplace?

A: It made him hot under the collar.

Tracy: Was your mom surprised when she got a rug for Christmas?

Trudy: She was floored!

Q: Why did Santa give Humpty Dumpty a lot of presents?

A: Because he's a good egg.

Q: Why did the snowman take a carrot to the library?

A: So he could put his nose in a book.

Q: How is Santa's beard like a Christmas tree?

A: They both need trimming.

Q: When does King Arthur do his Christmas shopping?

A: At knight

Q: How do dogs play Christmas carols?

A: On a trombone

Q: Why was the cookie so excited to see its family at Christmas?

A: Because it was a wafer such a long time.

Q: Why did the hotdog keep telling jokes at the Christmas talent show?

A: Because it was on a roll.

Q: Why did the snowman go to the dentist?

A: He wanted his teeth whitened.

Q: What happens when a polar bear is all alone?

A: He's feels ice-olated.

Peter: Do you think we should read a

    Christmas story?

Tyler: That's a novel idea!

Q: What happened when the elf showed up to

    work in flip-flops?

A: Santa gave him the boot!

Knock, knock.

Who's there?

Europe.

Europe who?

Europe late waiting for Santa Claus!

Q: What kind of bird is sad when Christmas is over?

A: A bluebird

Q: Why was the elf yelling?

A: Because he stubbed his mistletoe.

Knock, knock.

Who's there?

Cook.

Cook who?

Clearly the holidays are making you a little crazy!

Knock, knock.

Who's there?

Avery.

Avery who?

Avery nice person wished me Merry Christmas today.

Q: What game do elves like to play when they're not making toys?

A: Gift tag

Knock, knock.

Who's there?

Abby.

Abby who?

Abby New Year!

Q: How do snowmen make friends at parties?

A: They know how to break the ice.

Q: How do you get a polar bear's attention?

A: With a cold snap

Knock, knock.

Who's there?

Figs.

Figs who?

Can you figs the star on the Christmas tree?

Q: Why do you sing lullabies to a snowbank?

A: So it can drift off to sleep.

Tony: I don't think we'll finish our Christmas story on time.

Tammy: We'll have to book it!

Knock, knock.

Who's there?

Jewel.

Jewel who?

Jewel feel sick if you eat too many candy canes.

Knock, knock.

Who's there?

Left hand.

Left hand who?

I left hand forgot my scarf and mittens.

Knock, knock.

Who's there?

Wendy.

Wendy who?

Wendy snow falls, we can go sledding.

Knock, knock.

Who's there?

Sticker.

Sticker who?

Sticker presents under the tree before

Christmas Eve!

Knock, knock.

Who's there?

Rooster.

Rooster who?

Rooster turkey in the oven for
Christmas dinner.

Knock, knock.

Who's there?

Firewood.

Firewood who?

A firewood warm things up in here.